THIS BOOK BELONGS TO:

EGMONT

We bring stories to life

First published in this edition in 2017 by Egmont UK Limited
The Yellow Building, 1 Nicholas Road, London W11 4AN

Thomas the Tank Engine & Friends ™

CREATED BY BRITT ALLCROFT

Based on the Railway Series by the Reverend W Awdry
© 2017 Gullane (Thomas) LLC. Thomas the Tank Engine & Friends and
Thomas & Friends are trademarks of Gullane (Thomas) Limited.
Thomas the Tank Engine & Friends and Design is Reg. U.S. Pat. & Tm. Off.
© 2017 HIT Entertainment Limited.

HiT entertainment

ISBN 978 0 6035 7373 6
67525/1
Printed in China

THOMAS & FRIENDS™

Buzzy Bees

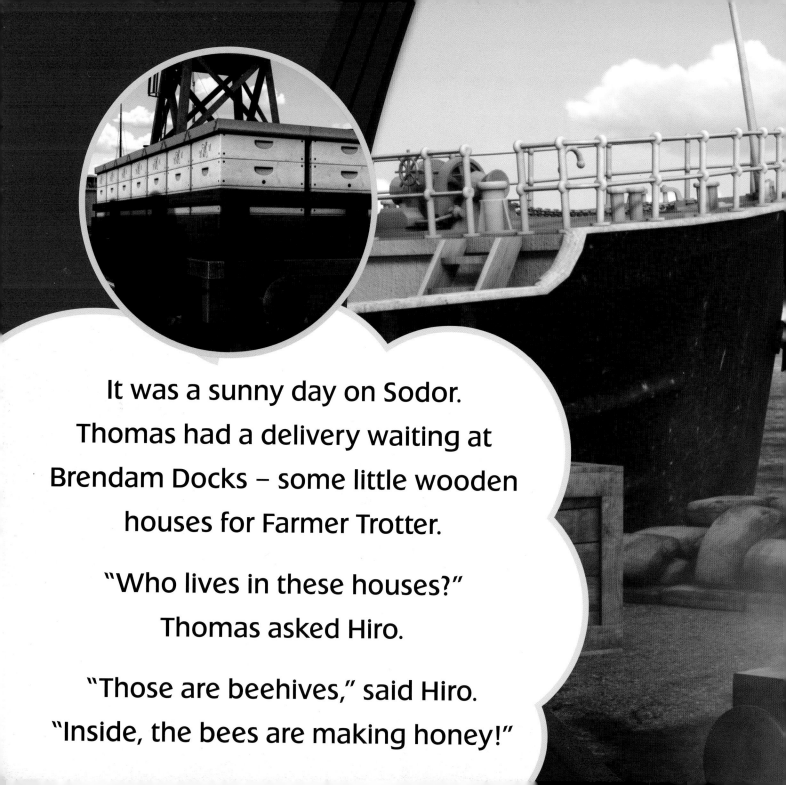

It was a sunny day on Sodor. Thomas had a delivery waiting at Brendam Docks – some little wooden houses for Farmer Trotter.

"Who lives in these houses?" Thomas asked Hiro.

"Those are beehives," said Hiro. "Inside, the bees are making honey!"

"I'll puff faster than fast to deliver the bees," Thomas peeped, excitedly.

But Hiro told him to go **slowly**. "Take the track through the woods so the bees can rest," he said. "I must pick up some flowers from Farmer McColl."

Hiro and Thomas both steamed away.

Soon Thomas came to a junction.

One track led through the woods.
The other track led past a field of flowers.

"The field is **prettier** than the woods,"
thought Thomas. "The bees will like that more."

So Thomas puffed off past the field.

Suddenly, Thomas heard
a loud *BZZZZ*!

The honeybees were flying out of
their hives and into the flowers.

"Oh no!" shouted Thomas.
"Come back, buzzy bees!"

An idea flew into Thomas' funnel.

"I'll **puff** to Farmer McColl's and pick up the flowers," he said. "The bees will **buzz** around them, then back into their hives!"

Thomas picked up the flowers, then chuffed back to the field.

When the bees saw the flowers, they flew out of the field …

… and all around Thomas!

They **flew** into his funnel …

… **buzzed** past his buffers …

… and **whizzed** round his wheels!

"Go away, buzzy bees!"
Thomas wheeshed.

But the bees were too busy
buzzing to listen to Thomas.

Thomas pumped his pistons and puffed away. But the bees would not buzz off!

"If you won't leave me alone," Thomas peeped to the bees, "then I will have to leave **you** alone!"

Thomas' Driver uncoupled his flatbed and Thomas **clickety-clacked** off down the track.

Thomas met Hiro at the next junction.

"Farmer McColl's flowers have gone," Hiro puffed. "And Farmer Trotter is still waiting for his bees!"

"Sorry, Hiro! I've done everything wrong," Thomas peeped, sadly. "I'll be as busy as a bee and I'll put everything right."

The bees were still **buzzing** around the flowers when Thomas collected his flatbed and *wheeshed* away.

The bees buzzed close behind.

Then Thomas chuffed back to the field. He collected the beehives and puffed off down the track.

When Thomas took the way through the dark woods, the bees began to feel cold.

With a **bzzzz** they flew into their hives!

Thomas puffed all the way to Farmer Trotter's farm. The farmer was so pleased to see his bees at last!

But Thomas still had Hiro's flowers.

Thomas sped back down the track
to where Hiro was waiting.

"You have my flowers!"
said Hiro, in surprise.

"I borrowed them to bring back
the bees," said Thomas. "Now the
bees will give Farmer Trotter the
best honey on Sodor!"

PEEP! PEEP!

The End

10 Thomas Storybooks

Join Thomas and the Steam Team on their fun adventures around Sodor!

Thomas and Friends™ fans will love this collection of colourful storybooks!

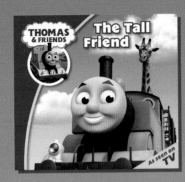

THOMAS & FRIENDS
The Tall Friend
As seen on TV

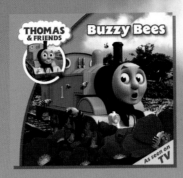

THOMAS & FRIENDS
Buzzy Bees
As seen on TV

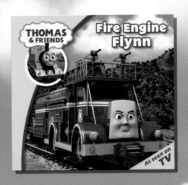

THOMAS & FRIENDS
Fire Engine Flynn
As seen on TV

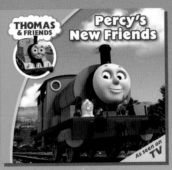

THOMAS & FRIENDS
Percy's New Friends
As seen on TV

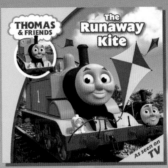

THOMAS & FRIENDS
The Runaway Kite
As seen on TV

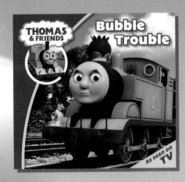

THOMAS & FRIENDS
Bubble Trouble
As seen on TV

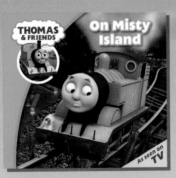

THOMAS & FRIENDS
On Misty Island
As seen on TV

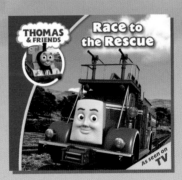

THOMAS & FRIENDS
Race to the Rescue
As seen on TV

THOMAS & FRIENDS
The Sounds of Sodor
As seen on TV

THOMAS & FRIENDS
Flash! Bang! Wallop!
As seen on TV